A Christmas Star

Written and Illustrated by

Leea Baltes

Special Illustration Contributions by

Ella Glinski

ISBN: 978-0-9986779-3-4

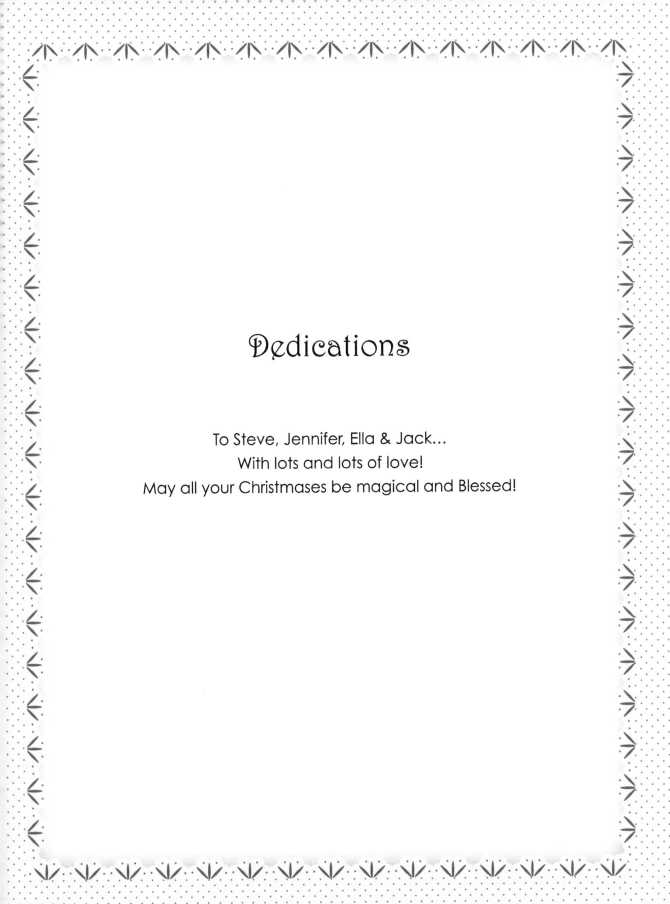

Dedications

To Steve, Jennifer, Ella & Jack...
With lots and lots of love!
May all your Christmases be magical and Blessed!

"*It's done!*" Jack yelled as he finished his star.
"The foil makes it the shiniest by far!"
He found the piece of foil down by the lake
and knew in an instant what he would make.

Mama held the star near the window's light;
it glistened and sparkled... and shone real bright.
Then she smiled, "Oh! It's so pretty indeed!
And it's just what our Christmas tree will need!"

"How will a Christmas tree fit in our house?"
asked Ella, the cute little worried mouse.
Mama laughed, "Don't you worry about that!
I know where to get one that's not too fat."

"We're all going up to Nana's house today
and, we'll pick out our tree along the way.
Nana still lives up by the old chicken coop.
She has a cold, so we'll take her thickened soup."

"*A sleep over!*" they squealed,
tugging Mama's sleeve.
"No… we cannot stay… for this is Christmas Eve!
So, get dressed real warm and let's get going.
We must be back before it starts snowing!"

But instead of getting dressed, like Mama said,
Jack stared at the star and scratched his head.
He wondered...
how would the star stay on the tree?
"*String!*" he yelled.
"*Tied real tight... it won't come free!*"

So, Jack added string... that went to the floor
and with star in hand... he ran out the door.
He wanted to see the star in the bright sunlight...
but, clouds moved in and made it dark as night!

A strong wind whirled and swirled all around;
picked up Jack and tossed him to the ground!
"Oh no!" the sad little mouse began to wail!
"No... no!" he cried as his star began to sail!

Mama rushed out as she heard her baby cry
and saw the star caught on a branch way up high!
The star was stuck, with its string all tangled;
high up in the hollow tree, it dangled.

Mama looked at the clouds with the threat of snow
and said, "*We can't get it now… we have to go!*"
She bundled Jack up in warm woolen clothes,
and all you could see was the end of his nose!

She quickly grabbed the jar that held the soup
and picked up her babies in one big scoop!
Then, off to Nana's they went in a hurry!
But, half way there, it began to flurry.

The babies shouted, "It's snowing! Hooray!"
They cried, "Mama, can we please stop and play?"
"No! No!" Mama yelled back. "We must not stop!
We must climb that hill and go over the top!"

They climbed the steep hillside of stone and roots.

The babies stayed warm in their homemade boots.

Their faces were red from the cold frosty air.

Mama yelled, "It's okay… we're almost there!"

They struggled and struggled... each little mouse.
Once at the top, they could see Nana's house!
She met them at the door with a hug and kiss,
and said, "*Shouldn't be out in weather like this!*"

"We wanted to see you, but we can't stay long;
we brought you some things
that will help make you strong.
Now, go get cozy in your chair." Mama said.
Then gave her hot soup served
with acorns and bread.

They opened their gifts with laughter and tears,
then all spoke of sweet memories...
down through the years.
They loved being with Nana on Christmas Eve,
and listening to the stories that she would weave.

The time flew by, and Mama knew they should go.

They all bundled up to keep warm in the snow.

Nana gave hugs, as she began to cry,

then, all blew kisses as they waved goodbye.

Once down the hill, Mama grabbed each little hand.

The wind blew so hard that they could barely stand!

The snow was so deep... almost over Jack's head!

So, Mama cut a pine branch to use as a sled.

She strapped her babies on with her shawl real tight...

and started to pull them with all of her might.

Against the fierce wind and the blinding snow;
Mama got lost... couldn't see which way to go!

"*I can't!*" she cried as the snow swirled around.

"I... *can't!*" she sighed...
as she collapsed to the ground!

But the mighty Heavens looked down upon her...
and whispered... *"Never give up ...*
never... never... never!"

Then...

The mighty wind began to slow...

the sky no longer dropped its snow...

the stars came out and looked divine...

and the frosty moon began to shine!

Mama looked up... at the moon shining so bright
and saw in the distance a small twinkling light.
She wondered what it was that twinkled so...
and then felt drawn... to its welcoming glow.

Mama picked herself up and with head held high...
"*I won't give up!*" she shouted. "*I've got to try!*"
With a new found strength...
she headed toward that light;
she was going to find home...
if it took all night!

She pulled that heavy branch... *inch ... by inch;*
through the deep freezing snow without a flinch!
Then... Mama noticed... after traveling quite far
that the twinkling light was ...

...Jack's Christmas Star!

"We're home... We're home!" she began to cry.
And then blew kisses to Heaven up high!

Mama got her babies into warmer clothes;
rubbed Jack's cold toes and kissed Ella's red nose.
She tucked them in and whispered,
"Always believe...
that you are truly Blessed on this Christmas Eve!"

Worn and tired, Mama did not stop there...
Tomorrow is Christmas... there's much to prepare!

"My babies will have Christmas by morning's light!"

She boldly declared ...
then worked all through the night.

The babies woke up and ran into the hall.

They crept down the stairs...

and peeked around the wall.

What they saw next was such a *surprise*...

they had to wipe the sleepies from their eyes!

Christmas had arrived in that very place...
and the joy could be seen on each little face!
The room was glorious from ceiling to floor,
with holly draped around the window and door.

The air was filled with the scent of fresh pine...
from their *branch sled...* held in a cork with twine.

No longer just a branch, that branch would be...
for now it was their beautiful... *Christmas tree!*

Then... from the kitchen came a yummy whiff...
their noses began to wriggle, twitch and sniff!
"I smell honey roasted thistle thorns!" Jack cried.
"And honey toasted acorns!" Ella replied.

They ran to the kitchen just in time to see...

Mama pouring *peppermint Christmas* tea!

"Merry Christmas, my sweet little ones!"
She sang while serving peanut brittle buns.

The babies gave Mama a hug and kiss...
and asked, "How did you do all of this?"

Mama smiled with a wink and a dimple...
"Christmas magic...it's really quite simple!
There's *magic* in the air on Christmas Day...
that creates *Joy* from all you do and say!"

They opened their gifts, while Mama had tea.

Then, they all snuggled up to look at their tree.

Mama told them about that first Christmas night...

about the *wondrous star* with its brilliant light.

"It appeared in the sky to show the way...

...to find a small Babe asleep in the hay.

Shepherds saw that star and heard angels sing...
of the glorious birth of a newborn King.
Wise men came to Bethlehem with gifts from afar,
they were led to the Child... by that shining star!"

Jack was sad that his star was still outside
and fought back tears that he could not hide.
Mama said, "Jack, *your star* is special indeed...
it helped us greatly in our hour of need."
Then, she smiled...
"That's how we got home last night...

...by your shiny star and the bright moonlight!

I really love your star way up in our tree...
and I think *that's* where it should always be!
And no matter how far away we may roam....
your star...will always guide us safely back home."

Then...after a little while...
Jack began to... *smile*.

The End

❦

Merry
Christmas!

Special Acknowledgements

Mom and Dad:
Thank you for making our Christmases special! My fondest memories are the wonderful cookies, the baked ham, Dad's decorations made out of tin foil... and just being together as a family.

Jennifer Glinski: My technical Designer.
Thank you so much for all of your hard work and talent that went into the design and development of this book. Just could not have done it without you!

Ella Glinski:
Thank you so much for your charming designs! You really gave Jack's star a delightful character!

And as always...
a big thank you to Mom, Alice, Rebecca, Alan & Sharon, and TK for your never ending support, encouragement and understanding.

To My Readers:
Thank you so much for your inspirational, positive feedback, your enthusiasm and your encouraging pleas for me to get this book completed. Your support has been greatly appreciated!

About the Author

Leea Baltes is an award-winning author, illustrator, and artist. Her passion for creative design began at a young age and is evident today not only in her children's stories and illustrations, but with her creations of fine art paintings, miniature 3D art, photography, costume, and jewelry designs. Her original works of art can be viewed on her website (http://www.leeabaltes.com), and online at Fine Art America and EBSQ, where she is a Juried Member. Leea lives in Maryland where she also enjoys nature's creatures, gardening, and her two cats.

Other Books by Leea Baltes:
Goodnight Wishes!

CPSIA information can be obtained
at www.ICGtesting.com
Printed in the USA
BVHW02n2313111018
529830BV00004B/20/P